# Steph

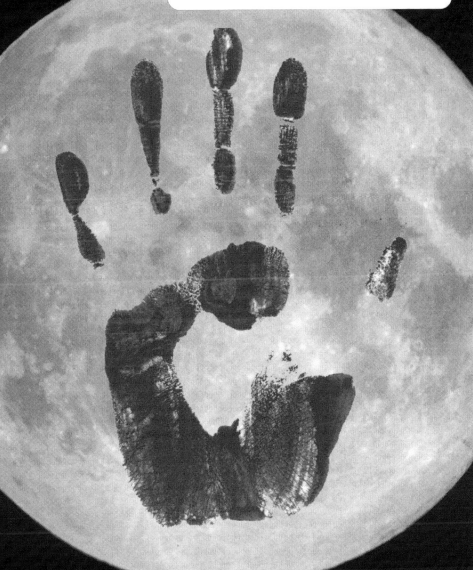

# Blood Rituals
## Crossroads Series III

# CROSSROADS SERIES: PART III

Three more short stories from the "Crossroads" series that will help keep you entertained late into the night. Discover the bright imagination, suspense, thrilling drama, picturesque visions, and the third look into the true meaning of the "Crossroads" series message.

Follow the series to piece together the hidden meaning in the stories to determine the overall message that is being portrayed. Will it bring enlightenment? Will it be the light at the end of the tunnel? Does fear take over and leave the message hidden? The journey continues and the message will surely begin to appear.

Copyright © 2014 by Stephen King

Manufactured in the United States of America
Designed by Magic Pen Designs

# Blood Ritual

Rain pummeled the front windshield of John Emerson's vehicle. It had been pouring like this ever since he left his house in Ashfield.

"This town must really hate me," he mused to himself aloud. Every time he took his vacation the heavens came down to earth.

He pulled off the bridge and towards the cliff's edge. This is where he had to be careful; apparently whoever paved this section decided it would be fun to make a slight incline towards the edge. Any sort of slip during this weather would send him sprawling through the barrier and into the abyss.

John eased off the pedal and the car came to a steady speed in which he was able to turn on the bend and move to the second bridge that led into town.

His eyes moved to the dashboard clock. He was only a few minutes out so he picked up his cell phone and clicked it on. He hit the contact at the top and waited a moment. When that moment was up he was greeted by an automated voice explaining to him how he had no signal whatsoever and should find a clearer area before dialing again.

Tossing the phone on to the passenger side chair, he peered out the window and smiled. He was on a bridge with nothing but the river beneath him, and no trees at all. How much clearer could it get?

Lightning struck somewhere ahead of him and reminded him that it was obviously the storm screwing with his phone. He shrugged to himself; he'd be at the house soon enough anyways.

In town he found that most of the places were shut down. A bar or two was still open, but it seemed as though the storm forced everyone into their homes. Not even the diners that took in passing truckers were open.

*This storm must have put the fear of God in people.*

The stop lights weren't functioning but since there weren't any cars on the road yet it didn't bother John. He pulled through the road, driving slowly, taking in the way the place looked without any life in it. He'd never seen it like this before. Even when he'd visited before the storms were never *this* bad.

John turned the corner and crossed the drawbridge into the residential district. The houses looked deserted. *Storm must have knocked out the power...* he thought as he made the turn and came upon his destination.

There was already a car in the driveway so John parked on the curb. He took a moment to gather his phone and overnight bag. Preparing himself for the onslaught of rain and hail, he opened the door and ran for the awning. The roofing above him threatened to come down on him while he fumbled for his keys. Finally he pulled out the one key he needed and slid it into the lock. John grabbed his bag off the ground, twisted the knob, and pushed his way inside.

******

Closing the door behind him, he set his bag down and unzipped his coat. He hung it on the rack and moved across the wooden floor to the kitchen.

The room was clean and organized aside from some pictures and notes stuck to the refrigerator. John made his way over there and opened the door. Inside was a plate of chocolate chip cookies with plastic over it. Smirking, he looked around him, making sure no one was there.

Once he was satisfied he slid the plate out and set it on the island counter. He grabbed a glass, some milk, and sat down on the stool at the counter.

He checked his phone while taking a bite out of the soft treat in his hand. Still no signal. Letting a slight sigh of annoyance, he put down the cookie and grabbed his bag. Plopping it down on the stool next to his, he unzipped it and pulled out his laptop.

Flipping it open he noticed the internal clock displayed that it was nearing four in the morning. He blinked in surprise; time had got away from him. He thought about getting some sleep, but passed on the notion. He had plenty of time to do his job here so there was no rush, plus he was enjoying his cookies too much.

Letting out a yawn, John stretched out his arms and began pulling on the cuffs of his green long sleeves so that they were a bit roomier. Focusing on the laptop in front of him, he moved the mouse and opened up some files he had stashed on it before he'd left his house. He was glad he had the forethought to put them directly on the machine instead of trying to download them once he got here.

Resting his chin in his hand, he began reading over the documents he'd written a few days ago. He had already memorized them, but with power out and nothing better to do it didn't hurt to be a little more prepared.

******

John looked up from the computer and checked his cell phone. The time was quarter to five in the morning. He rubbed his eyes and put his hand on the laptop.

"You're here?" said a voice behind him.

Half awake, he thought he imagined the voice and ignored it.

"John?" This time he turned around. A woman stood behind him looking as awake as he was.

She scuffed the floor on her way over to him. She wore a black long sleeve outfit that seemed too large for her and when she wrapped her arms around him; her arms were hard and small.

"I didn't want to wake you so I stayed down here," John said shutting the laptop slowly.

She kissed him on the cheek and moved from the island to the fridge. "You found the cookies I see." She said noticing the empty plate and glass with a mild smirk.

John smiled shyly. "You didn't want any did you?"

She raised an eyebrow. "I don't eat that stuff remember?" She opened the refrigerator door and started to rummage through it.

"Right, right. Sorry, I forgot… long hours…" He took a deep breath, rubbing his eyes more, and then letting his hands fall down on the table. "What are you doing up anyways?"

She pulled out a juice box and lifted herself on to the island. "Storm woke me up." She poked the straw through the box and started to sip.

John smirked, "Well try as it might this town can't keep me out."

She looked outside, the hail had lessened, but the pelting noise was still loud enough to be heard. "So who is it this time?" she said with the straw hanging off the side of her lip. She poked the laptop.

"Now, now," John said with sly tone. "You know I can't tell you that."

She rolled her eyes, "I know, I know, the whole 'less you know the safer you'll be' deal."

"Exactly." John picked up his laptop and headed over to the living room couch. Sitting down he set the laptop down on his favorite coffee table. He didn't open it though as his companion sat down next to him and promptly laid her head on his lap.

"Here, lift your head up." He slid a pillow under her head and laid his head on the back of the couch, giving his eyes a rest.

"Will you have to go to work tomorrow?" she asked quietly.

John started running his fingers through her darkening auburn hair. "Partially, it's mostly research until Tuesday. I'm going to visit Marcus at the store though. Do you need anything?"

There was a moment of silence before she responded, "I'll get you a list before you leave."

He nodded and set his head back again, continuing to slowly run his fingers through her hair.

******

When he woke up there was a growing pain in his neck. Groaning, he tried moving it around and was rewarded with sharp pains. He took a deep breath and eased into turning his neck. The muscle still struggled, but didn't hurt nearly as much.

"You're awake, finally," a familiar voice said to him from behind. Those same bony arms wrapped around his neck.

"What time is it?" John asked after a yawn.

"A bit past eleven." She gave him a quick kiss and walked back into the kitchen. He followed suit, searching through the cabinets for a heating pad.

"Did you get that list ready?" he asked pulling a pad out and tossing it in the microwave.

She handed him a slip of paper and a cup of coffee. He took the paper but passed on the coffee. "Sorry, not today," he said while placing the heating pad on his neck. "I need to be alert; being hopped up on caffeine isn't going to help me."

"But you barely got any sleep." She grumbled.

John looked at the clock again as he went for the door. "Six hours is plenty,"She gave him a look and he sighed. "I'll be back soon and I'll take a nap then, ok?"

She nodded and waved, "Be careful."

"Always am!" he called as the door shut.

He started to walk off, stuffing the list in his pocket. He stopped then, realizing he was missing something. John backtracked to the house and was about to turn the knob when the door opened and an arm extended holding his wallet and his camera.

He smiled, taking both and giving her a kiss. She smiled, "What would you do without me?"

John smirked and set off again, waving behind him.

******

The storm had given up and now only a dense fog remained in the air. John needed to remind himself of the lay of the land, so he passed on using his car. The bridge wasn't too far from the house and getting from there to the shopping district was only a matter of minutes thankfully. He could use the exercise anyways.

With his hands planted firmly in his pockets he crossed the bridge without a single car passing by. He did his best to not let it faze him, but there was a sense of strangeness that he couldn't shake. Where was everyone? The town was usually so busy it would take you a good twenty minutes to cross the bridge.

He took a moment to pause and admire the lake below him. He took the camera out of its bag and aimed it at the lake. For whatever reason he couldn't get it to focus on the lake.

After struggling to get it to focus, he clicked the button to take the picture. At the last second it decided to focus on the fog and snapped the photo.

Sighing, John looked at the photo he took. Fog. *Wonderful.* The more he stared at it though, the more it looked like there was a shape in the fog. He blinked and shut the camera off, resolving to examine it on his laptop later.

******

He made his way off the bridge and into the shopping district. Despite looking like a heavily trafficked area, there was no one in sight. None of the stores on the block were open. John knew power was back because the streetlights had been turned on. So someone was doing their job.

He knew the quickest way to Marcus' store was through Crichton Street, but as he approached the intersection with Koontz Street, he noticed a gaping hole in the road. He peered over the edge, but the fog made it impossible to see any sort of bottom. He knew the storm was bad, but to think that lightning could have caused this was unbelievable.

*Maybe there were tremors in this part of town?*

When he looked up again he saw that the pavement was intact near the General Store, so he just had to find a way over there now.

He turned down Koontz Street, passing the barred entrance to the hospital. John paused to admire the establishment that had once been so respected. It was easily the best hospital in the city, which is until the head doctor got involved in a nasty drug scandal.

Suddenly a lamp flickered inside the courtyard. It stayed lit for a moment before winking out of existence. A second later the light across from it lit up. John stared at it. The place hadn't been used in years. The only thing that surprised him was that the city hadn't cut power to it yet.

Moving on past the hospital, he turned the corner on to Canyon Street and was welcomed by a wall of skin-colored cloth. Confused, he saw that it spanned the entire length of the road. There were hazard signs lying on the ground near it too. Assuming it was there to keep people away from the construction, he turned back, getting slightly frustrated.

John turned back on Koontz and noticed the pharmacy. Wondering if he could find a back door to go through, he jogged over to the door and pulled on the knob a bit. The door budged slightly. An idea popped into his head. He took out his wallet and slipped a credit card under the lock, wedged it a bit, and then lifted. The door clicked and he was inside.

The place was deserted of course, so John just strode through. He was looking for a door that led through the back. Maybe the place where they took and off loaded deliveries would work?

He finally made his way around the corner and found the door he was looking for. This one, if anything, would lead into the back. Unfortunately for John, it was locked via a keypad. *Naturally*... Now he had to find the code. There were only a few places it could be kept.

John paced around somewhat aimlessly before he spotted the manager's office. There could be worse places to check first.

The room was an utter mess. File cabinets were knocked over; papers were everywhere. The computer had been smashed and desk turned over. *They just couldn't make it easy could they?* Sighing, he started rummaging through the files on the ground, looking for something that would have the code written down on it. His only hope was that it wouldn't be on the computer. Otherwise he'd be stuck here for a while.

About five minutes into his search it dawned on him that he was searching for a needle in a haystack. This was pointless. He sat down, looking aimlessly around the room.

There were posters, a picture or two of the family. One of the pictures was a portrait that hung behind the chair. An older man with a round face and balding head sat against a regal looking backdrop. John could only assume that it was the manager. He smirked at the idea of the guy thinking his job here was so important that he had a portrait of himself made.

John stood up to get a closer look. He hadn't seen it in the dark, but as he got closer he noticed that the guy's eyes were crossed out in red. Whoever had done it clearly didn't like this guy. John made a face and turned back to the room. He saw that the answering machine was blinking red. He pressed the button.

"You have one new message," said the automated voice. "Recorded five, eight, two-thousand nine." *Beep!*

"Hey! It's me! Yeah I remembered your birthday this time," the message began. The voice sounded oddly like his, but just different enough you could think it was someone else.

"I mean, how could I forget? It's the big four-oh! Anyways, your gift is in the mail, you should get it in time for the party, see you soon!" Click.

John's lips perked up. Could it really be that easy? He moved over to the picture of the parents, looking closely at the father. He was smiling proudly next to his son at graduation.

He moved back to the keypad and slowly pressed the numbers in. *Five, eight, one, nine, six, nine.* There was a satisfying click and the door slid open. John let out a sigh of relief. He could barely contain himself from letting out some kind of crazed laughter as he pushed the door open and stepped through.

The delivery station was barren, not a truck or box in sight. He was beginning to wonder if someone had looted the place during the storm. Either way, he strode through quickly and made his way to the shutter. He lifted the shutter up just enough for him to get through and then set it down quietly once he was on the other side.

Satisfied that he triumphed over the town's numerous ways of impeding his progress, he moved down what was left of Canyon Street and turned on to Midway Avenue.

John stepped carefully, wary of any tricks the road might try to play on him. As he passed he noticed how all the stores were closed. Some of them even had signs posted in front displaying that they were closed because "inclement weather". *Yeah and an earthquake,* John mused to himself as he continued onwards.

He turned passed the floral shop and jogged over to the General Store. Thankfully there was no sign out front and the lights were still on so he grabbed the handle and let himself in.

The place smelled like meat waiting to be cooked, one of John's favorite smells. He walked up and down the aisles as fast as possible. He was afraid that somehow everything would disappear in front of him if he didn't hurry. After all he'd seen already, he didn't blame himself for overreacting. When he was done he headed over to the butcher counter where he could get the last of his list.

The counter was unmanned so John rang the bell. "Marcus! You back there?" He rang again. "Marcus!"

He heard the cranking of a steel door and felt a rush of cold air fly over him. "Hold on, hold on! I'm coming! Jesus Christ Almighty..." Marcus stepped out of the freezer, taking off his gloves as he approached the counter.

"John! It's good to see you, how've you been?" he said with a toothy smile. Marcus was a plumb man with no neck and a mustache that looked like his kid drew it on with a pencil. He always looked like he got a little too carried away with his meat. His apron was always smothered in blood.

"I've been good, Marcus. You?"

Marcus waved in the air, "Ah, can't complain. You know me! Same shit day in, day out, everyday. There is always plenty of meat to cut! You know what I mean?" he said with a hearty laugh.

John smiled uncomfortably. "Yeah, I do." *More than you know.* "So how's the wife?" he asked to steer the conversation in a more manageable direction.

Marcus eyed him. "You never ask about my wife." John noticed Marcus' fingers start twisting around his wedding ring. "Why the sudden interest?"

John raised an eyebrow. "What are you talking about Marcus? I always ask about Deborah."

"You haven't asked about Deborah since she died," Marcus spat at him.

Figuring out that he made an awful mistake, he just quickly asked for his order. Marcus took the list and grumbled all the way back to freezer and then out again with the packaged meat. John thanked him, paid, and left as fast as he could.

*What's wrong with me?* He couldn't believe he forgot that Marcus' wife had passed away three years ago. He'd have to be more careful next time. That's *if* Marcus ever let him back into the store again.

He went back the way he came and made his way to towards the bridge. He was so distracted by his mistake that he didn't notice the rabbit in front of him until he almost stepped on it. It looked young and had grey fur.

"Oops." He said bending down in front of it. "Hey there little guy. You're a long way from home." The only place in town where there were rabbits was the Elementary School and that was at the far end of the Residential Area. Perhaps it was a wild one?

He reached to pick it up. Instead of running away, or even coming towards him, the rabbit bit him. Recoiling, he realized there was something strange about the rabbit. Its eyes were black, he couldn't find any color in them and its fur seemed to have a red tinge to it. It didn't look anything like the cuddly creature he'd found a second ago.

John reached for it again, and this time the rabbit backed up and fell over. It squirmed, trying to right itself. John put his arm out to help it, but it tried to bite him again. After a moment more of struggling, it went stiff as a board. John poked it carefully, wondering if it was trying to put him in a false sense of security. But no matter what he did it wouldn't budge.

So John stood up, brushed himself off, and went on his way. He tried his best not to ponder everything that had happened today and did what he could to look forward to going home, cuddling up with his best friend, and forgetting the weirdest day of his life.

******

He was so distracted with his thoughts that he didn't even see the girl rounding the corner until he was on the ground, staring up at her wide, blue eyes.

"Are you ok? I'm so sorry, I cut the corner too quickly" she said in a sweet tone. Her wavy hair was black as night and blew in the breeze gently.

John took her hand and stood up, shoving his groceries back into their bag. He hoped desperately that his embarrassment didn't show in the dark.

As he checked for everything he felt something damp press against him. He realized after a moment that the girl was carrying coffee. He then realized that that coffee was all over him.

"Sorry about the shirt too…" she said shyly. She was dressed in a red hoodie and looked no older than seventeen. Even so, John, who had lived here for several years and visited even more after that, had never seen anyone jog this path before.

John quickly debated how to respond and figured he'd had a bad enough day already and didn't need any more trouble. He smiled, "I'm fine, don't worry about it."

"You sure?" she said.

"Yeah," he nodded. "Thanks though."

She smiled, "Great. I'm Juliet by the way." She held out her hand.

*And here comes awkward conversation number two…* John swallowed his sigh and shook her hand. "John."

"Well, *John*, I'm sorry. Again."

"Really, it's alright." *Leave me alone, girl.* He looked up to sky for help and felt a rain drop pelt the back of his neck. *Thank you,* he said silently to God.

Within seconds the skies opened up and rain began pouring down on them. "Crap! I better go. See you around!" Juliet threw the hood over her head and took off past him. Not wanting to be stuck in the rain forever, he took off in the opposite direction.

******

John made it back to the house as quickly as possible, dropping the groceries on the island counter and making his way to the bathroom. He took a towel and dried himself off. After he pat down the craziness of his hair, he went into the living room and flopped on the couch. He lay down, rubbing the sides of his head.

"How did it go?" his favorite voice said to him.

"Awkwardly." He responded without looking back.

"What do you mean?" She came by the couch with a glass of water and two pills. Grateful, he took them and sat up to swallow them.

"Did you know that Marcus' wife died three years ago?" he asked as she sat down next to him.

"Of course," she said. "We went to the funeral. I remember you telling me your theory on Deborah's convenient death. You remember don't you? It was pretty ridiculous at the time. You went on and on how he killed her in order to draw business to the store."

*That's right.* It was all coming back to him now. "That reminds me." He said opening up his laptop. He quickly typed in a note about Marcus' schedule and closed the window.

"What?" she asked him.

John took the camera out of his pocket and popped out the memory stick. He loaded it onto the computer and showed her the image of the fog he took. "I took this at the bridge on my way to the store. Do you see this?" he traced the lines of the human looking shape with his finger.

She giggled, "It looks like a bunny!"

"What?" He said in surprise.

"See! There are the ears," she pointed to two pointy areas. "And the tail." She pointed again to the opposite side of the picture.

John saw it then. "Huh." He said, examining the photo again. "What do you know?"

"Oh, I got something for you," she rushed back into the kitchen and came back with two folders. He recognized the numbers at the top as a case number.

"You went to the station?" he asked, setting the folders on his lap.

"It was pretty easy since it was closed," she answered sitting next to him.

"I'm impressed." He really was, as getting into the station even while closed wasn't easy. It's something he had never personally tried, but was willing to give it a go now.

He opened the top folder and took out a photo. The picture was of a man on the floor with his chest cut open like he was autopsied. And that was just putting it lightly. Blood was everywhere.

He flipped through more papers and saw that the boy was only eighteen years old and had recently graduated high school. He noted that the lead detective was a Douglas Hellard. *Why was Shephard's Glen involved?* "Did they ever find out who did this to him?" he asked curiously.

"Yes. But there was never a trail because that was the mayor's kid. He must have paid people off to sweep it under the rug. The news said it was an illness."

"Fascinating." He said while going over more photos. "So tell me, who was it?"

"His girlfriend, Clara Millson." She answered.

"Crime of passion?"

She shook her head. "No, she claimed she was raped and that she killed him because of it."

"What makes you think she was lying?" He set the photos down, completely enthralled now.

"Because of this," she pointed to the second folder. "In there are reports of other killings, all just recently graduated, all eighteen years old."

"Don't tell me," John was getting excited. "Same M.O.?"

She nodded. "They never found any evidence linking these to Clara, but I wouldn't be surprised if you dug something up."

"These are only the ones the police have found as well." He said picking up the new stack of photos. "The mayor's son was killed three years ago. I wouldn't be surprised if there were more."

"What are you going to do about her?"

He stacked the photos neatly and inserted them back into the folder. "I'm going to wait." He said putting the folder on the table. "I have other business to attend to."

"You mean the reason you're here?" she asked, clearly curious.

John nodded and stood up. "Tomorrow though. Right now, I need a nap," and with that he walked off towards the stairs.

\*\*\*\*\*\*

The next day his head had stopped pounding and he was all ready to go. Climbing down the stairs, he headed into the kitchen and said his goodbyes, grabbing his overnight bag on the way out.

John put the bag in the trunk of his car and got in. He sat there for a moment, wondering how he was going to get back to Marcus' shop when the roads he tried to take before were closed off or sunk in.

He opened the glove compartment and pulled out a map. Looking it over he found a route that would take him to the store, if it didn't have anything blocking his path. Setting the map on the passenger seat, he turned the keys in the ignition and took off down the road.

It was a long drive as he had to constantly stop and look ahead to make sure he wasn't going to drive off into the abyss. Fortunately there didn't seem to be any obstacles this time around and he finally made it to Crichton Street. Pulling up to the curb he shoved the map back into its proper place and got out of the car.

The fog hadn't gone away yet but for once it served his purpose. Taking the bag out of his trunk he looked around him and took off behind the building.

Marcus was in so the back door wasn't locked. He unzipped his bag and pulled out a cord. He wrapped one end around the tip of his palm and zipped the bag back up, leaving it near the wall.

He prowled quietly through the storage area, carefully listening for any approaching footsteps. Nothing so far. He continued through towards the freezer door. Noticing the control panel near the door, he flipped the panel open and started to increase the temperature. *Better to get started now*, John thought as he closed the panel and moved on.

He peeked in at the main area and saw that Marcus was tending to a customer at the desk and pulled back behind the wall. He waited impatiently for the customer to finish paying.

"There you go Mr. Hellard." Marcus said. John caught his breath, listening closely now. *Hellard.* "If you don't mind my asking, why are you here?"

There was a pause; John assumed that Hellard was choosing his words carefully.

"I needed some fresh air, Marcus. It's hard being cooked up in that town after Ethan and Peter left us. Mary's taken it hard and…" he trailed off into silence. *Sounds like my lead detective has a few secrets that need uncovering…*

Marcus broke the uncomfortable silence, "Don't worry about it. I won't say anything to anyone." *That's right you won't,* John smiled to himself.

"Thanks, Marcus. I'll see you later." John heard the bells ring as the front door opened and closed.

Now was the time. He only had to wait for Marcus to go check the meat in the freezer, which if yesterday was any example, was every time there wasn't a customer.

Sure enough he heard the pounding footsteps of Marcus coming towards the hallway. John held his breath, as he needed absolute silence now. Marcus took a step in, and stopped, and his hand went to his chin as if he was trying to remember something he'd forgotten.

Whatever it was passed over and continued on. John let the other end of the cord hang and he gripped it tightly with his right hand. Slowly, he crouched down and followed Marcus.

He turned the bend towards the freezer and noticed the panel. "What? Who the hell touched this? They'll ruin my meat!" he yelled to thin air. This is when John struck. He stood up, wrapping the cord in between Marcus' chin and chest, pulling as tightly as he could.

Marcus was a big man, but he was slow and made mostly of fat. There was no way he could resist what was happening; as much as he tried. After one final tug on the cord, Marcus' arms fell limp and the rest of him followed. John untied the cord, panting as he retrieved his bag from outside. When he came back he quickly flipped the front door sign to 'closed' and locked the door.

He opened the freezer door; the temperature hadn't lowered enough for the meat to smell yet. He dragged Marcus inside and closed the door. Then he opened his bag. He had work to do.

******

Marcus' eyes popped open, darting from end to end of the room. John rose from his meditative pose and loomed over Marcus. "It's about time. I thought I was gonna be here until next April." He smiled and paced around the meat slab that Marcus was bound to.

"You know," he said bending down to eye level. "It took me three years to find proof that you murdered your wife."

Marcus tried to protest but the gag in his mouth preventing him from doing anything but breathing.

John resumed his pacing. "I went over everything again and again. Finally it hit me." He turned to face Marcus. "You framed your assistant. It was the only time in the twenty years you owned this store that you ever hired someone else."

John shook his head, smiling. "It was a genius plan, you know. Teaching him how to carve meat so his cuts would look identical to those on your wife's body. Making sure he didn't use gloves so his fingerprints would be all over the knife. But that's all circumstantial isn't it?"

He stood over Marcus and reached into his pocket. From it he withdrew a ring. "Your wife's wedding ring was never found. The police assumed your assistant took and hid it, waiting for the heat to die down before he sold it. It makes sense except for one minor detail." He paused for dramatic effect. "His prints aren't on it. Yours are."

"You might be wondering how I got the ring. Well, it's quite the story, one I don't exactly have time to tell you. But it helps to have someone on the force, you know?"

Marcus started to squirm. He tried to scream, but only muffled sounds rang out. "There's no point in struggling, Marcus." John withdrew his favorite knife from bag. "It's over."

He plunged the knife into Marcus' chest, savoring the moment as the life drained from his body. He took a deep breath, lifting the knife out. He wiped it clean and set it down, preparing for the next phase of his ritual.

"Hey! Anyone home?" said a voice from outside the freezer. John looked up, still as could be. The sign said closed and the door was locked so he was hoping whoever it was would just give up after a few tries.

"Something smells in there. Is everything's alright?" The voice was feminine and John could swear he'd heard it before.

She knocked again. John then heard the clicking of a lock. She had a key and here John was in an open freezer with a dead man on the table.

He had to think of a plan, fast. There was no way he could pack up and escape with everything. Plus there was Marcus' body and there was no way he could get rid of that without being spotted. Leaving the body here either was pretty pointless, that would alert the town and the whole idea was to be unknown.

Unfortunately it seemed like that wasn't going to last long. So John was forced to come up with one final plan. He grabbed his knife and waited by the wall next to the door.

"Marcus, are you here? I think your meat is rotting." John closed his eyes in disbelief, as the voice was Juliet's.

She pulled at the door. The handle was large and got stuck pretty often. This could have bought John more time if he had any kind of plan other than killing her when she stepped in the room. Now all it was doing was causing him anxiety. He hadn't planned on killing more than one person today, let alone someone who didn't deserve it. But plans change.

After another hard tug the door pulled open. She gasped. She ran inside just enough for John to grab the back of hair and pull her towards him.

"Quiet." He said holding one hand over her mouth and the other with the knife to her throat.

Her breathing steadied and he dropped his left hand. "John, what is this?"

John smirked. "Don't play games with me, Juliet."

"But… why?" she sounded more curious than frightened.

"Let's just say our good friend Marcus got what he deserved."

"Are you going to kill me too?" she asked; now she was scared.

"Perhaps."

She started to shake. "Please! I'll do anything!"

*What a loaded phrase.* John didn't have any reason to kill her, but he couldn't just let her leave either. He had to find a way to keep her quiet. Then the idea sprang to him. It would be torture, and beyond scarring. But it might just do the trick so he wouldn't have to take yet another life today.

He brought her over to his bag, bent down to put it on the table with Marcus' body and opened it up. "You said you'll do anything as long as I don't kill you," he stated, rummaging through the bag.

He withdrew a bone saw. "Be careful what you wish for." He handed it to her. Her hands were shaking so badly he thought she was going to drop it.

"What do you want me to do with this?" She said in almost a whisper.

John smiled at her then at Marcus. "Cut him up. We can't just leave this here. Someone will be come looking." He gave her a wry smirk.

She didn't protest, or say anything for that matter. She knew that if she wanted to get out alive she would do as she was told. "How?" She asked.

"It's as simple as it sounds. The smaller the pieces, the easier it'll be for you to package them."

"What?" She said.

John motioned to the bag. "There's a set of garbage bags in there. Use as many as you need to take care of business here."

He was hoping that the experience would traumatize her so much that her mind would just block it out and he would be forgotten all together. It was a long shot, but it was his best bet at the moment.

He gave her a clear welding mask to wear and his leather apron. He then took a step back and watched as she began. The process was slow, but even more so for her because she was shaking so much that the saw almost went through other parts. As time went on though, her hand got steady and her breathing calmed. John noticed that she wasn't scared anymore; she was calm, as if she was enjoying it. *Fascinating.* He thought as she continued. *Adrenaline is a funny thing.*

When she was finished cutting she carefully began to package and string each bag, setting them neatly in a corner. When she finished completely she set the drill down and took the mask off.

Her eyes had bags under them, as if she hadn't slept in days, and her skin had paled but her expression was otherwise normal. John couldn't believe that someone could endure that and not be crumpled in the corner crying to themselves. *Well, someone normal,* he thought to himself. Perhaps there was more to Juliet than he initially assumed. He made a mental note to study her further and sent her on her way.

\*\*\*\*\*\*

He stuffed the bags in his car and drove down to the lake. There he loaded the bags on to the boat that was always docked. When he was done he turned on the light at the end of the dock, got in the boat, and took off towards the center.

The lake itself had an eerie history, just like the town it was located near. But today the fog gave it a quiet, serene feel. The fog also served as natural cover for John as he dropped the parts of Marcus' body into the liquid abyss. The water swallowed them, grateful for the meal.

He dropped the last bag into the water and followed the light back to the dock. He secured the boat and looked back to his car; except it was gone. Confused, John searched around. No matter how hard he looked, there were no cars parked in the lot.

Then it hit him. Like an idiot, he'd followed the wrong light and wound up on the other side of the lake.

Shaking his head he headed towards the mainland and sure enough after a few minutes he was right next to the Historical Society.

He headed back to the dock to find that the boat had disappeared completely, rope and all. The town was screwing with him, he could feel it. Frustrated, yet determined, he set off back to the road, trying to think of an easier way to get back to his car other than walking around Toluca.

Unfortunately nothing seemed to be presenting itself so he resolved himself to at least trying to enjoy the walk back. The road was long and almost no one used it, he could use the time to think about his next endeavor: Clara Millson.

He managed to make it only a small part of the way back before he ran into a large gate blocking his path. He looked around and the gate didn't seem to be an entrance to anything specific, it was just "there". He shook it. Locked. It was too tall to climb so he turned around. There was another road; he would just have to cross the entire town to reach it.

Giving into the futility of attempting a shorter route, John set off on the road in to the southern side of town. Just like the other side of town, the place was completely deserted. While he didn't mind the peace it was slightly off putting to find that every inhabitant of the town had just up and disappeared. Then again, when he looked at the buildings the windows were closed and the doors were barred so it was possible everyone was inside, it just didn't seem likely.

The walk was a quiet, yet long one. He wished desperately that a stray cab would come by and he could hitch a ride all the way back to the other side of the lake. The route wasn't made to be walked.

At the same time he was thankful he was alone because he was freaking out about someone stumbling on to his car. He'd hidden his bag of tools in the trunk, but if someone went snooping it wouldn't be too hard to find them.

That thought sent John into a jog across the road that went around the side of the lake. It was getting dark, and the streetlights didn't appear to be working. If he didn't hurry, he'd left out in the blackness. He did his best not to think of what would happen in the dark on a day like this.

As he made his way down the road he noticed a blinking light straight ahead of him. It was the only source of light he could see. It seemed to penetrate the fog and threatened to blind him with its brightness. He had no choice but to put his hand in front of his eyes and step carefully as he continued.

He hoped for a fleeting second that it was a car or a motorcycle approaching. But the light never seemed to get any closer to him. It only seemed to get brighter and hotter.

John could feel himself sweating from the heat of the light. His throat became rough and the sweat burned off his brow. Every time he swallowed it hurt. He was in dire need of the water. He had no idea if he was making any progress at this point.

His head was light feeling and he was no longer stepping in a straight line. A second later a ringing started in his ears. He covered his ears and bent over, his jaw clenched in pain. He couldn't stand straight and fell to his knees.

John had no idea what happened next. But he went blind and deaf, and the darkness enveloped him.

******

When John woke up, he was shaking. It took him a moment to realize his body wasn't in shock or anything like that.

"Wake up John!" That female voice was yelling.

John blinked and put his hands up. "I'm awake! I'm awake!" He called. She stopped shaking him and let him go.

"What happened to you?" she asked. Her face was concerned. She looked like she hadn't slept all night.

John sat up. It took him a moment to realize that he was back in the house. He looked at her and wiped his face. "I have no idea." He looked around, his eyes wide. He felt panicked. He didn't know what was going on.

"John." He felt her cold hand on his cheek. It felt nice. His body was still cooling off from whatever happened last night. "Talk to me."

John refocused on her. "I have no idea." He told her. "I did my thing. Went after Marcus and took care of business there. Then there was this girl… Then when I went to dispose of the mess, I wound up on the wrong side of the lake. I tried walking back but…" He rubbed his eyes and tried to clear his head.

"There was this light. I don't know where it was coming from. But it was hot… I couldn't see…" He looked around once more, wanting to make sure that this wasn't a dream of some kind. "How did I end up back here?"

She shrugged and wrapped her arms around him. She gave him a soft kiss on the forehead. "I have no idea. I was worried when you didn't come back. But then a few hours ago there was this loud bang on the door and I found you collapsed outside."

John wondered who, if, anyone would have brought him back home. There was Juliet, but she had no idea where he lived – hopefully.

"It's been a very weird few days," John commented, yawning. His body felt stiff, like he hadn't moved in days.

"You mentioned a girl." She said. "Did she see you?"

John nodded. He didn't want to worry her, but he couldn't lie to her either. "She wound up in Marcus' shop. I tried to keep her out but she was persistent."

She sighed and sat back. "Did you have to kill her?"

John shook his head. "I thought about it. But instead I made her cut Marcus up." The words were just flowing at this point. He didn't understand it. He usually tried to keep her out of his side of things. But it was proving difficult today.

"And that worked?" he was asked.

John shrugged. "I hope so. She disappeared after that. But it was odd." He said, thinking back to Juliet's reaction back in the freezer. "She was upset at first. But as she was doing it she… became focused? I don't know. She was remarkably calm after a few minutes."

"Interesting." She said. "Maybe there's another one out there like you?"

John's head snapped to look at her. "No. I definitely don't think that's the case."

She placed a cool hand on his cheek and massaged it with her thumb. "Aw, don't be jealous. I'm not going to replace you."

John smiled faintly. "I need to go get my car. It has all my things in it." He stood and went to find his shoes.

"Are you sure you need to leave already?" she asked.

"If I don't do it now I'm just begging for someone to find it. Even though this whole town has been deserted for days. I don't get it. What's happened to this place? First the earthquake, then the construction, now everyone is gone! There's the fog, the lights. I'm feeling worse than I ever have before. It's not supposed to be like this when I come here." He tried to catch his breath. Slowly it calmed down, but he realized he was beginning to sound like a madman.

"I think you just need some proper sleep. When you get back you can come upstairs with me. Then you won't have anything to worry about." She flashed him a small smirk.

That sounded nice, John thought. He tied his shoes and went to the front door. But what he saw stopped him in his tracks.

"What is it John?" She asked, joining him at his side.

On the front porch was a note. In big bold letters it said: "TEACH ME". Lying next to it was the body of the rabbit John had seen on the bridge. It had been cut open and used as the writing material.

Right beside the note was his bag of supplies. The car hadn't been returned, but when John checked through the bag, everything was there.

"You need to find this girl." She told him. "Do what you have to. Teach her, kill her, I don't care. But you need to make up your mind."

John nodded. He'd need to travel light while tracking someone. So he took the small digital camera and a single knife. Then he disappeared into the fog.


The signs were clear. Whatever he'd done had triggered something inside of Juliet. She'd snapped and was coming after him. Whatever she wanted though he wasn't sure he could give. He'd never taught anyone before and he honestly wasn't sure that was the best idea. He needed to limit his exposure. The more people who knew about him the more likely he was he would get caught.

He followed some wet shoe prints for a few yards before they disappeared on to the main side walk. John hoped it wouldn't be too hard to follow her from there. After all, there only seemed to be three or four people in the entire city.

He was lucky when he hit the sidewalk and he knew it. There was a trail of blood, hopefully only the rabbit's. He followed it for as he long he could. It went over the bridge, through several roads, and even through the back of the pharmacy. Had she been following him all this time?

John was beginning to wonder if this was more than just a single rabbit's blood. He shuddered to think what was actually going on.

Eventually it led back to the lake. Back to the parking lot where his car was. The trunk was open and sure enough, Juliet was standing near the passenger side door.

"You found me." She said with a smile.

John did his best to contain his sarcasm. "It wasn't difficult." He took a step forward and splashed against something. He looked down and saw that it was a small puddle of blood.

"Where did you get all this?" He asked her.

"Do you really want to know?" She asked, taking a step towards him. John stepped back and noticed that the entire parking lot was layered in blood.

It looked like some kind of sick art project. He could see that the blood made a full circle and that there were other intricate designs further into the circle.

"What is this?" John asked, finding it difficult to keep this cool.

Juliet took another step towards him. She brandished a knife, one that looked similar to John's. "This is the ritual we need to complete. Since I know you won't teach me, I have to kill you. It's only custom."

John blinked. "What are you talking about?"

"Surely you completed the ritual yourself. I did some reading on it after our little encounter at the freezer. You have a handler of sorts I assume?" Juliet's smile was stretching her face. It was beginning to look a bit Cheshire.

"I'm sure you've seen the signs. The ones that prelude this. The lights, the visions. When you forced me to cut Marcus up you started something. You set into motions forces beyond your control."

John drew his knife, wondering if he should make a run for it. But something was keeping him here. This nagging need to finish what was started was overwhelming him, no matter how hard he tried to fight it.

"At first I wasn't sure if I wanted to go through with something like this. But the more I read, and the more I thought about what you made me do, the more I realized this is what I'm meant to do."

John shook his head. "Look, I don't know what you think is going on here, but these blood rituals are not a part of it. You can stop this."

Juliet shook her head. "No, I can't." She took another step towards him and held the knife tight in her hand.

They began to pace each other. John didn't want to kill her. She hadn't done anything to deserve it. But he couldn't leave. He couldn't run. No matter how hard he tried to force himself to do so, he wouldn't leave. He was stuck in this twisted circle.

Juliet stabbed at him. She was clumsy and her momentum nearly sent her sprawling to the ground.

"Leave, Juliet." John said. "I won't tell you again." He looked at her. She was so young, so pretty. She could have a life. "I don't want to kill you."

"It's over for you John." She told him as she righted herself. "There's nothing you can do to stop this. The ritual is only fulfilled when one of us is dead. You know it, or else you would have left."

John nodded. "That doesn't mean you can't leave. You initiated it. You can put an end to it."

Juliet shook her head. "I won't do it."

John took in a deep breath and put his feet in a fighting stance. "I'm sorry."

The duel was short between them. Knives aren't exactly weapons made to go against one another. Their short, meant for small, quick attacks. There was no clashing of blades or sparks of battle.

There was simply blood. They each got hits on the other. John found himself surprised each time the knife would find its way into his body. But he kept going. Adrenaline was keeping his body active and the ritual was propelling him forward.

He tried to stop himself. But at this point he was running on nothing but the ritual. It had taken control of him. It was forcing him to finish this. Nothing short of complete and utter victory would end it. Surrender on either side was not an option.

Juliet was better than she had initially let on. He wondered briefly if forces beyond his control were helping her, making her faster, stronger.

In the end it didn't matter. In a swift flash it was over. John hadn't realized it at first. It happened almost too quickly for him to register. He blinked and saw that the knife had left his hand. It lay of the asphalt beside him.

When he looked down he saw that Juliet's knife was wedged between his ribs. He spit up blood, unable to speak.

"I would apologize." Juliet said. "But this is your own fault."

John's mind registered little else after that. He saw the ground meet him head on. He noticed how the blood that made up the ritual circle had cooled, practically soaking into the ground.

Darkness claimed him after.

******

Juliet wasn't sure what had brought her to this house originally. There was a sense of being drawn there. She hadn't been able to understand it at first. But now that she was here again she felt complete.

The house looked brighter than the last time she'd visited. Perhaps it was the fact that the fog was gone now and the sun was shining. Either way it was definitely a more welcoming sight than before.

As she approached the house she saw a shape in the distance. It was definitely a human. As she got closer she could tell it was a young woman. She was maybe only slightly older than Juliet. She wore a long black sweater. Her arms were so small they looked like bones. Her hair was long and auburn. It covered half her face. Her eyes had dark circles under them.

Juliet approached quietly and carefully.

"It's alright, child. Don't worry." The woman said. Her voice was soft and comforting.

Juliet came closer and smiled. The woman came over to her and held out a hand. Juliet took it. It was cool to the touch. She took a step forward and kissed Juliet on the forehead. She was shorter than Juliet had expected.

Then she moved in and gave Juliet a small kiss on the lips. She smiled shyly and led Juliet into the house.

"It's time you begin."

# Rafflesia Road

I was about fourteen years old when I first heard about Rafflesia Road. It was about twenty minutes outside of the town of Waynesboro, TN where I grew up. It was like a lot of the stories that you hear about when you're growing up. It was a lot like those legends that adults would tell you to keep you in line. My papa used to tell me the one about old man Lester who supposedly murdered his family in the 1800's. We had about eighty acres of land; in the very back of it, in a tiny field there was an old green shack where he supposedly lived.

He would say, "George, don't let Old Man Lester catch you poking around that old house in the back forty acres. You'll become his next victim."

Well, that story worked until I got to be about eleven or twelve. That's when I went back there to see for myself. The shack was just that- a shack, have caved-in and fallen apart with vines engulfing it like some extraterrestrial plant. It looked too dangerous to enter; so I didn't try. What was really interesting was what caught my eye in back of the shack. The sunlight glinted off of something in the woods in the hollow behind the shack. When I went to investigate, I found poppa's moonshine still sitting there in a dark woodland glade. I had me a nice sample from it too. I had to walk it off for a couple of hours before I could go home. So, you see most legends are stories adults concoct to keep you from doing one thing or another. That is except the legend like Rafflesia Road.

The Rafflesia is the largest flower in the world. It's big, red and beautiful and it grows deep in the rainforests of southeast Asia. It entices insects to pollinate it with its rotting smell. That's why Indonesians call it the 'corpse flower'. It's quite a fitting name for such a place. We first started hearing reports about people coming up missing who'd supposedly last been seen in the area of the road. It would be one or two people every couple of years. The FBI even came down to check it out in the late 80's and came up with squat. Then, the next week after the investigation, one of the agents returned to the road and disappeared. Again, the agents returned to check out the scene; but found nothing but a pretty place on the edge of the woods.

You see, Rafflesia Road is on the edge of a Wildlife Management Area called Eagle Creek. It's a non-descript gravel road that runs beside a meadow, which is often full of blooms in the spring and summer. On the edge of the meadow is a beautiful creek that borders the Wildlife Management Area. It would be the ideal spot for an afternoon picnic if there weren't something more sinister at work there. As I said before, I was about fourteen when I first heard about the place; my friend Timothy and I were anxious to check it out, although our parents told us to stay away, of course.

We borrowed (without permission of course) Tim's dad's rusty Ford pickup and headed out there one sunny afternoon. I brought some of poppa's moonshine along just to stave off the boredom. We got right in the middle of that gravel road and stopped. Nothing stirred except the breeze in the trees that bordered the meadow. We got out and walked to the place where the road ended. Still nothing was happening; but I do remember thinking it was just about one of the prettiest places in Wayne County that I'd ever seen. The meadow, creek and the backdrop of remote, wooded hills sat together almost as elegantly as any Ansel Adams photograph. Where the road ended there was a sign marking the borders of the Wildlife area and a path leading off into the woods. We stopped there and passed the flask back and forth a few times. We woke up with Tim's dad standing over us with a look that might stop a bear in its tracks. All we gained from that first trip was a hangover and a beating from both our poppas that made it awful hard to sit down for two days.

Things changed when I got to be sixteen. I wasn't much concerned with local legends by this point-- I was off chasing Freda Johnson, the hottest girl in the whole county who wouldn't give me the time of day because I didn't play football or hang with the popular kids. It was one afternoon when I got home from school that things would change for our family forever. My younger brother, Carl was known to throw colossal fits when he did not have his way. He had his eye on a certain dirt bike for months and told poppa that's all he wanted for his eleventh birthday. Well, times were real lean for us during this period; and when that birthday came around, poppa had no bike for Carl. Carl threw a fit and climbed way up in the live oak tree that used to be in our front pasture. He climbed up to the furthest reaches in branches that would have snapped under the weight of a full-grown adult. Poppa came out and told him to stop being childish and come on down. Carl, of course, being Carl refused. Then, Poppa finally gave up and went in the house. He figured that Carl would probably get cold and hungry enough that he would come down before bedtime. Well, a storm came up from the south and the wind began to blow something fierce. We ran outside when we heard Carl yelling. He was trying to come down from the high branches when the wind really began to toss the treetops.

"Hold on, Carl, I'm coming to get you!" I yelled as I began to climb carefully up towards where he was hanging on. I was getting real close to where he was when the wind kicked up again and Carl lost his grip. I reached up to grab him, but I couldn't quite reach him. He fell to the ground and did not get up again. It tore me and Poppa up more than words can say. Poppa cut down that old tree the next week so he wouldn't have to be reminded of what happened. Momma had already left us four years previously and now this. I didn't see Poppa's eyes much after that when they weren't glazed over with the spell of whiskey.

Later that same year I returned to Rafflesia Road. I decided to go there to get some of my studies done; it was such a quiet, scenic spot and I knew that I wouldn't probably be disturbed there on account of the legend surrounding it. So, I spread out a blanket, ate some of my Aunt Clarice's fried chicken and started to read my book. I remember specifically it was Catch-22 and I had to have it read by the end of that week. I got about one chapter in when I saw something very strange happening before my eyes. There, between me and the edge of the woods, was that old oak tree that used to be in our front pasture- my hand to God! I was amazed and perplexed to say the least. I walked up to the tree and tried to rub my eyes but it was still there. Then, I looked up in the tree; much to my disbelief I saw Carl! He was in that same place he had been on that fateful day, trying to hang on when the wind was tossing him around like a kite. I began to climb up just as I had that day. I wasn't sure what was happening exactly; but I knew that I had to try and save Carl again if I could. I got all of the way up to where Carl was and even grabbed a hold of his coat. Just as I did so, some kind of opening appeared just above me and began to pull me into it.  It was like the swirling in the clouds you see when a funnel cloud is forming. I let go of Carl and began to move back down the tree. I could still feel the pull but I closed my eyes and concentrated on getting out of the tree.

"This is NOT real!" I said to myself as I neared the ground, still feeling the pull; but less so. Then, just like that I was back on the ground again and the tree was gone. I knew then, that something sinister was happening on Rafflesia Road; although I wanted to get to the bottom of it, I knew that I did not want to return there. I went over the events in my mind and thought about the difference between the first time I visited the road and the second one. The only real difference I could think of was Carl's death. Something about that trauma had activated that place--had created some kind of opening that was trying to suck me into it. I had no understanding of what it was; but I knew it was something I had to avoid. I decided to keep the whole incident to myself. I knew that no one would believe me; not even my best friend, Tim.

Well, later that same year I got my first car--it was a beat-up old Chevy Nova that didn't look like much, but it was packing some horsepower. It was also around that time that I met my first real girlfriend, May Hawkins. She was one of those shy girls that wears glasses, but when she took them off and lifted her head, you realized she was just about the prettiest thing you've ever seen in your life. I began to talk to her in our Physics class when I should have been paying attention to the lesson. She didn't talk much at first, but I broke down her resistance after a while. She was impressed when I gave an interpretation of a Longfellow poem in our English class. The guys turned and looked at me like I was some kind of leper, but May came right up to me after class.

"That was real eloquent what you said in class," she said.

"Aww it was nothing," I said, trying to appear macho and not into reading and stuff.

"I love it when a guy can take literature and art seriously," she said.

"Oh, art and literature is my thing too," I said, upon hearing her response, knowing full well that I was full of it.

We began talking and hanging out after school from that day forward. A couple of weeks later, I asked her to the drive-in and that's when I laid a kiss on her. She blushed and smiled, but I knew she was feeling the same way I was--like I was walking on air. Well, after we really started to get to know each other, we began to share some of our personal traumas. Turns out, May had an uncle named Marty that she was real close to and loved like a father. Her real father was an alcoholic that rarely showed any kind of real love for his family. May would go over to her uncle's house at every available opportunity. What May didn't know was that her uncle was suffering from severe depression, which he masked when he was around his family the best that he could. One night when May came over for a visit, she found her uncle very drunk and depressed. She did her best to console him and tell him everything would be ok; he insisted on being left alone and made her leave. She begged him to let her stay; but he wouldn't. Later that same night, her uncle Marty put a shotgun in his mouth and ended it all. That was when she was thirteen years old. She told me she couldn't help but think there was something she could have said or done that might have changed his mind. I told her I knew exactly how she felt. This was one of the things that we shared in common was our personal tragedies.

The whole incident at Rafflesia Road began to rear its head in my thoughts again. After a few months, May and I went to one of our favorite spots near the Buffalo River. As it got late and after we had a few cold ones, I found myself talking about Rafflesia Road again. I told her about the tree, and Carl and the strange opening. She was intrigued and enthralled with my story. At first, I didn't expect for her to believe me; but she trusted me and knew that I was telling the truth. She asked me where the place was and said she had heard about people coming up missing in the past. There was Shawn Able who went to school with us during the elementary years. There was Sharon Tate from Hohenwald that disappeared when I was an infant. I told her there was something not right about the place and that I would never go back there again.

About three days later, I could not get a hold of May. Her parents told me that they were very worried because she had not returned from school the day before. She would always drive directly home from school in her mom's Chevy Cavalier and wouldn't go anywhere else without calling them first. It was just not like her at all to disappear like that. They began to suspect that someone had abducted her outside the school or somewhere. The next day a search began around the school grounds. I searched longer and harder than anyone else in the surrounding area; but there was no sign. May's parent filled out a police report and the search continued for two days with no results. Posters were put up; the community was put on heightened alert. That third day it dawned on me where May had gone.

I jumped in my Chevy Nova and headed out to Rafflesia Road. When I got there, I sat and waited in that same spot that I had sat down on before; sure enough after a few minutes I could see the old oak tree again. I could hear Carl calling for help from the topmost branches. I climbed up the tree again, just as I had done before until I almost could touch his hand. Once again, the clouds began to swirl like a twister was coming on and the opening began to pull on me. This time, I didn't resist and I was picked up and sucked into the opening. When I opened my eyes, the swirling clouds that were all around me were gone. It was pitch black all around me; and I could hear some strange sound like machinery operating in the background. I noticed a little light coming from the far side of the room I was in., so I moved towards it. When I got there, I realized that I was in a holding cell of some kind, although I was alone. On the far side of the room there were steel bars; or at least I thought they were steel. They were constructed of some kind of metal that I hadn't seen before- they had a strong luster to them. I put my nose through the bars and yelled out,

"Hey! Anyone there? Open up this cell, right now!" Just then I noticed the cells across from me had people in them that came into the dim light to see who was making all of the noise. Just across from me was May who flashed me a smile and waved.

"Don't worry; I'll get us out of this. I'm not sure what's happening; but I'm going to get to the bottom of this."

"Oh sure you will," said a voice from the cell next to May's. "Sorry, the name's Kevin--. I've been here a little while now, but I know my day for the draining is coming."

"The draining?" I asked him.

"Yep. Sooner or later they will be feeding off your anxiety and guilt that you store," Kevin replied.

"What anxiety and guilt?" I asked.

"Well I don't know that; that's your personal business. Here's the deal: We are all here because we brought something they feed off: usually it's some trauma in your life that you harbor extreme guilt over."

"Who the hell is this 'they' you're talking about and how the hell can someone feed off of feelings.

"Well, you have a lot to wake up to, don't you? They always do when they first get in here. Oh, it's all a dream, this couldn't be happening. Poppycock! Reality is much stranger than we ever gave it credit."

"I see," I replied. "That's a lot to take in but I would definitely prefer that this was a dream."

"So what do you know about what 'they' are?

"Beats the hell out of me--my guess is that they are some undead creatures from another plane of existence to which they have transported us. We are one of their 'farms, where they can extract our energy like a cow's milk."

"That's not a nice thought," I said, looking down at my shoes.

"You're about to meet the 'they' I'm talking about--look sharp!" he said.

A tall, hooded figure walked or should I say floated into the room. There was no appearance of feet beneath the long cloak and no face or form, only darkness beneath its hood. It turned towards my cell and the door swung open. It held its hand up and I felt mesmerized suddenly and knew I was supposed to follow; it was like it was using its will to command me. May's cell opened and she followed right behind me. We were guided out of the dungeon-like cell area and into a wider space that had a very futuristic feel to it. We were floating along with the hooded figure down a corridor suddenly and saw several other hooded figures sitting down as if they were working; but I couldn't see any computer screens or any ordinary office equipment. There were only figures sitting as if meditating; but focused like they were concentrating. Then we passed another room where there were ordinary people in these strange chairs with luminescent lights that seemed to be lighting up as if they were receiving energy from the people sitting in them. Some of the people looked drowsy as if it were making them sleepy and others less so. One hooded figure hovered at the opposite end of the room as if it were monitoring the proceedings. Finally we came to the end of the corridor into another wide-open space. There, two hooded figures put us on a machine that was a futuristic version of weight scale at a doctor's office; but this one had lots more light and I could tell, was taking more information from us than our weight. A few minutes later we were whisked back down the hallway and back into our cells.

"So, what were they doing exactly?" I asked Kevin through the bars.

"They were processing you. They were recording lots of basic physical information to add to their database and some that no human doctor could ever record. It's unlike any database you've ever heard of- thousands of times larger."

"Processing us for what?" I asked.

"Recording information for their studies mostly and assessing the health of your anxiety if you will. That's what they will harvest eventually. I'm getting close to my draining. I can tell because of the energy I've gained back since the last one. You feel really sleepy and weak at first: that lasts several days sometimes. Then they allow you to sleep extra and recuperate. After you get back up to normal speed, drain again. Problem is human beings can only be drained of their anxieties so many times before they can no longer give energy to their machines. Then you are useless to them."

"What happens then?" I asked.

"What do you think?" he asked making a hand motion like he was slicing his throat.

"How do you know all of this?" I asked skeptically.

"I've been here a little while. Let's just say I'm a keen observer.

They were silent for a few moments as another hooded figure hovered through, stopped for a second and moved on.

"So is there any way out of here?" May asked as she curled up near the entrance of her cell.

"Yes, I'm glad you asked that question. I know where they bring the new people in: it's the opening you have to go through to get back to your entry point: at that goddamn road whose name I won't even utter. We have to make a break for it when the opening occurs and resist the will that the hooded ones will impose on you. That won't be easy."

"So how do we know when the opening occurs?" I asked.

"We don't, but it's been long enough now for the next one to occur."

"You mean they bring people in that often?" I inquired.

"No, they actually come and go out of it. Where they go and what they do I have no clue," he answered.

"You guys are the first they've taken in a pretty good while."

Another figure came down the hallway and raised its hand. Our voices went silent, again controlled by its will. We felt suddenly sleepy and went and got in our cots. The next morning, we were brought food that somewhat resembled what we thought of as food. Kevin was red-eyed and jittery. He had actually stayed up almost all night practicing resistance to their will. He turned to me and began to talk to me and May who came to the front of her cell to talk.

"Listen, you guys have to practice resisting their will if you hope to escape when the time is right," he said. "I've been practicing and I'm happy to say, I'm getting better and better at it, even though I pretend to follow their will so they won't suspect anything."

"How do we practice?" May asked.

"You have to project your own will. I know it sounds weird, trust me; but after a while you learn to do what you need to do. When you feel your own will being taken over, you resist and will something different- whatever it is you want to do.  So, if the hooded ones will you to follow them, try resisting the next time. Oh, and another thing: they will be coming to extract your energy soon. You need to act tired, like you are not up to full strength yet. It worked for me the first time anyway."

The next morning came around and we tried what he said. It actually worked for a few seconds, but then I found my own will taken back by theirs when they willed me to walk to the showers. We practiced this for about three days, noticing how our resistance to their commands was getting easier. We would fall in line after resisting so that the hooded ones wouldn't notice. The hooded figures never uttered a word or did anything out of their routine they were almost robotic in nature. One of the figures came to my cell at an odd time when they didn't usually come. Kevin observed what was happening and nodded to me. I immediately lay down on the bed and coughed. I even held my stomach and pretended like it was upsetting me.

"Is there any way you could get me something for my cough?" I asked the figure. It turned from the cell and began floating back down the corridor. Another figure came to May's cell later that same day.

"Remember what Kevin said, "I whispered loudly.

She moaned in the bed and blew her nose like it was stuffed up, rolling over like she was about to go back to sleep. The figure watched for a second, then moved on down the hallway.

"Nicely played!" Kevin said, smiling through the bars. "It won't work every time though; I want to get you guys out of here soon so you never have to experience the draining. It's an awful feeling."

"What's it like?" May asked.

"Like you were forced to run four miles as fast as you can; that's how drained you feel. The one thing that I can say is you are too exhausted to worry about what got you here in the first place."

"What did get you here if you don't mind me asking?" I inquired.

"I don't mind. I had a gun that I used to keep in my closet, but I always kept it unloaded. One day after taking it hunting I forgot to unload the last shell in it. My little brother, Andy shot himself accidentally playing with that gun."

"You didn't mean for that to happen," May said.

"Yeah, it's always the same- everyone in here knows in their heart of hearts that some things are beyond our control; but all of us are haunted by what we could have done to prevent the inevitable. I could have locked the closet. I could have removed that last shell. What are you gonna do?" he said, solemnly.

Finally, on the next day- it happened. Just before we were to be taken to breakfast, we saw two of the hooded figures hovering towards the corridor where the openings occur. Kevin caught sight of them first as he scratched his stubbly beard and his eyes widened.

"C'mon, George, C'mon May--get ready. They are gonna come get us for breakfast at the same time those two are headed out the opening, if they come on their regular time! Remember, resist and make for the corridor where the opening is as soon as they open your gate."

Sure enough two cloaked figures came to lead our cellblock to the dining hall. This would be the time when our will would be tested. The hooded figures were going to try to lead us in the opposite direction to the opening site, so we would have to resist. As soon as Kevin's gate was opened, he was off without any trouble, making for the opening. One cloaked figure went in pursuit, while the other continued to open our gates. May was let out, but she stood there behind the figure as if she couldn't resist its will. I could see from her expression that she was really trying. Finally, I got out and grabbed her. It was hard resisting and I thought it would split my skull in two, but we finally made it down to the end of the corridor. One of the cloaked figures appeared out of nowhere and tried to grab us. We managed to get past him to where another hooded figure was standing next to an extremely bright opening at the edge of the room. I looked closer and realized that it was the opening and I could see the swirling clouds on the other side of it. We had to assume that Kevin had already gotten through and the figure must have gone after him. The cloaked figures reached for us with their invisible arms, but I lunged straight into the opening, holding onto May.

We fell right through the swirling clouds and landed right where I had seen the old oak tree. We had to lie there a minute because the impact of our landing was a hard one. Afterwards we got up and ran towards my car as quick as we could. When we got to the car we looked up at the opening, which had narrowed. From it we could hear Kevin's voice.

"They've got me: run for it!"

We got in the car and rode off as fast as we could. We never went back to Rafflesia Road, not even to get May's car. It was something that only we would talk about when no one else was around. We would never know who the cloaked phantoms were--if they were extraterrestrial or from another dimension or if they were undead wraiths. Whenever we did talk about it, our minds would go back to that day when we escaped; we would shake our heads and say what a shame it was about Kevin and the others that never made it out. We would get married in three years' time and have two children of our own, Richard and Gina. They never knew our story about the road. Someday someone might read this diary and know my account of that place; let it be known by that reader that I consider myself of sound mind. No, I never shared this story once with anyone- but people still tell tales about the Rafflesia Road on a dark, autumn night by the fire. It's the road that attracts the emotionally damaged, like the flower attracts insects with its odor that smells of rotting corpses.

# Intervention

Davis Stevenson was an artist who was looking to find isolation. He had just recently divorced his wife, Carla who had had an affair with his good friend, Steve. His life of late was filled with emotional turmoil; his idea of therapy was to throw himself into his work and get away from all of the noise and distractions of the city. As a matter of fact, he had moved out of the house that he had lived in with his wife in Nashville. He had just answered an ad in the paper about an old country house that was for rent way out in the sticks. It was a white, Victorian-style country home that had just been newly painted on the outside. The inside was fully furnished with the same furniture that had been in the house for many decades. Behind the house were forty hilly and wooden acres except for a small overgrown garden in the back of the house. A little creek wound around behind the garden. It was the picture of isolation and there weren't any neighbors for many miles around; just more hills and woods.

Davis set up his easel in the front room near the hearth. He thought this room would provide the most inspiration because it was full of very large windows that allowed it to become illuminated by the morning sun. He felt that in this setting, he could almost pretend that the past did not exist and begin life anew. Just as he began to make a few strokes with his oil paints on the canvas, there was a knock at the door. It was Mary Walton, the seventy-four year old owner of the house. She had lived in the house for many years with her family but was now the only one still alive. When Davis opened the door, she smiled and held out a fresh pie that she had baked.

"Hi Davis, I just wanted to see how well you were settling in and if there was anything that you needed," she said.

"I'm settling in just fine, Ms. Walton. I was just getting ready to begin work on a new piece but I appreciate your visit and the pie," he said taking the pie out of her hands. "Would you like to come inside for a minute?"

"Eh, no dear, I have some errands to run in town, I better not," Davis noticed that the expression on her face seemed to change when he mentioned coming inside and he thought that to be very odd. "Please let me know if you need anything; if anything is, eh, well, not to your liking give me a call, anytime," she said as an awkward smile came across her face.

"Thanks Ms. Walton: I sure will," he said and then he closed the door. *She is very nice, but somewhat odd,* he thought to himself, going back to the canvas. Oddly, his paints were now on the mantel instead of the chair were he left them. Also, his brush was on the chair; before he went to answer the door he swore he left it on the edge of the easel. *Hmm must need a little more coffee to wake up my brain* he thought to himself. As the day wore on, the painting began to take shape. He was becoming inspired by his surroundings and letting his imagination have full rein. The painting showed a doorway with a shadowy figure standing in it. On the opposite side of the painting was another shadowy figure on a bed positioned as if the figure were bracing itself upon seeing the figure in the doorway. Davis wasn't sure where the idea had come from like many of his paintings; but he liked the mystery of the potential conflict between the two figures. He used a swirl of blue, gray and white oil paints that gave it almost a Van Gogh-like quality.

Late that afternoon, he was satisfied with his work and decided to take a nap on the couch. His bedroom was upstairs, but he didn't feel like climbing the stairs. He always felt a sense of confidence and relief when he was making progress on a good piece of work. Although the tension of the recent events in his life was still present in his conscious thought, they had receded to the background. He laid down on the couch that was covered in what appeared to be an antique quilt and closed his eyes. He quickly began to slip into a dream. In the dream, he thought he was waking up from the nap. He got up from the couch and began to walk towards the downstairs bedroom that was in the back of the house. Davis had no idea why he was being drawn to this room. When he entered the doorway, it was as if he had passed through a silvery mist. The sensation he felt was somewhat like your funny bone feels when you hit your arm just right, but it was all over his body. Once he passed through the silvery curtain, the sensation stopped and he looked around him. On the small bed in the corner there was a young teenage girl who looked to be seventeen or eighteen. She was lying on the bed staring towards the doorway with an anguished expression. A wheelchair sat just at the foot of the bed. Davis thought that she was quite beautiful with her big, blue eyes and long brown hair that fell around her neck. He wanted very badly to ask her what was wrong, but could not bring himself to form the words. From where he stood to the left of the door, he noticed that a shadowy figure was entering the doorway. As the figure came into the dim light, he saw that it was a middle-aged man with unkempt hair and a stubby beard wearing overalls. His expression was one of drunken lust and Davis could smell the stale liquor on his breath. The man approached the bed where the girl was lying and she seized up into a ball, wrapping her arms around her legs. The man suddenly was on top of the girl forcing her to unwrap her arms. His arms were pressing down on hers and he was holding her down with the full weight of his body. He was wearing a sinister grin and began to tear at her shirt to try and remove it from her body. "NOOOO!" she cried as she tried to struggle, but it became apparent that she was overpowered by his greater strength. Davis attempted to yell at the man to stop, but found himself waking up instead. Oddly, he had woken sitting in a chair in the bedroom instead of the couch where he had fallen asleep! David was really disturbed by these events. As he looked at the painting, he knew that the figures in his creation were the same ones in the dream. He wondered what the hell was happening to him and why he had woken up in a different place from where he fell asleep.

That night he had trouble getting to sleep because he could not get the peculiar events of the day out of his head. Finally he drifted off to sleep. In the middle of the night, he awoke to a sound that seemed a lot like a soft whisper coming from the edge of his bed. He knew it was probably another dream, but when he heard the voice again, he knew that he was awake. The voice whispered, "Please, help. Help me, Davis." This left him quite disturbed and he quickly got out of bed and searched around the room and the adjoining hallway but there was no one there. He did however feel quite a draft just inside the doorway, but could not for the life of him figure out how the cold air was coming. The windows and doors were all shut tight. Finally after a lot of staring into the darkness of the bedroom, he got to sleep.

The next morning he debated about whether or not he should call Ms. Walton and tell her about the events that had transpired. He decided that it must be the tension of recent events that was causing these strange dreams, but he could not figure out why they were manifesting themselves as a young girl seeking help from someone who was obviously trying to molest her. After an hour or two, he decided to get back to work. He wanted to complete four more pieces for his art show in two months and wanted to get to work. Davis decided to put the piece he did yesterday aside and start a new one. It disturbed him a little too much to look at it. He got out the oil paints and began on a fresh canvas. This time the picture depicted a room that was stacked with cans and old furniture. His hands painted two figures again as if there was someone else in control of their motion. This time one figure was at the end of the room with a finger on a light switch. The other figure was the girl in the wheelchair on the opposite side of the room. Once he finished a couple of hours later he looked at it and felt the same disturbed sensation again. Why was he depicting these same figures? Why couldn't he paint something else? It was then that he realized that some outside force must be guiding his will. Davis exhausted himself with these thoughts so greatly that he fell asleep on the couch again.

Getting up from the couch in the dream, he walked across the house to the stairway near the kitchen that led to the basement. He walked down the stairs and opened the door. Once again, he had the sensation that he was being pricked with pins and needles and he passed again through a silvery mist. Once he was at the bottom of the stairs, he realized that it was quite dark. He did see the shadowy outline of what he assumed was probably the man from the previous night's dream at one end of the room and the shadowy figure of what he assumed was the girl sitting in a wheel chair on the opposite side. The standing figure began to walk slowly towards the girl. Davis could see that the standing figure was also holding something that might have been a gun; it was too dark for him to know for sure. "NOOO PLEEEASE!" the girl yelled as the figure drew closer. Again, Davis attempted to intervene but instead awoke from the dream to find himself in the basement. The figures were gone and the light above him was on. His eyes were drawn to the far corner of the room where a wheelchair was folded up. That night, he did not sleep; he just stared into the gloom. He was afraid of having another disturbing dream with the handicapped girl and the creepy old man. Just before dawn, Davis was staring out of the window towards the back garden. He swore he saw the translucent figure of the teenage girl sitting in her wheelchair in the yard staring up at him. Her expression was forlorn and full of grief. He backed quickly away from the window and rubbed his eyes as if he were trying to wake up from another dream. Davis looked out of the window again; this time the girl was gone, but he heard her voice again in the room coming from the space above him. "HELP! PLEASE HELP!" A short distance away, he heard the sound of evil laughter. He was pretty sure it was the creepy man he saw in the girl's bedroom.

Now he was quite disturbed. Because the same phenomenon had happened twice, he knew that something very strange was at play. Either he was going completely mad from the stress of recent events or something really otherworldly was occurring. He decided to get out of the house for the day and meet his friend Charles for lunch in the nearby town of Kingston Springs. Charles was pretty open-minded and could give his interpretation of the events that had occurred.

"So how's the painting coming along?" Charles asked after taking a bite of his burger.

"Fine. I have two pieces that I've completed already," Davis answered.

"Wow, that's quick. Can I see them sometime?"

"Sure, they are not quite complete but you can come out and visit soon," Davis answered seeming a little anxious when he said the part about coming to visit as if he were desperate for company.

"Charles. I need to tell you something in confidence, but please don't tell anyone else," David said softly.

"Ok, sure. What's up buddy?"

Davis filled Charles in on all of the events that had taken place the past couple of days and didn't spare any details.

"Wow, that's quite a story. I would be upset too, buddy," Charles answered. "Well I know one thing for sure: you are about the sanest guy I know so I'm pretty sure you aren't crazy. Besides, I believe in the supernatural as you know. It sounds to me like the girl is trying to reveal something to you and needs you to help her. My guess is that she must have died in that house."

"And the man that I saw is the one that must have killed her," Davis said finishing his thought.

"Yes, that was what you were about to witness in the basement," Charles said.

"Whew, I knew I was sharing this information with the right person. Thanks for not asking me if I feel ok or any of that crap," Davis said, feeling better about the situation already.

"Sure man. Look, I know this woman who is a friend of my moms. She supposedly has the 'sight' or whatever. She's been known to predict things that have happened and to be able to communicate with spirits and such. I will give you her number," Charles replied.

"Thanks- you are a true friend buddy," Davis said, clutching the number like his life depended on it.

The woman's name was Sandy Barnes. She was well known in psychic circles and more than willing to help. Davis tried to offer her money, but she said she would not accept it. This gave Davis confidence that she was the real thing and not some scam artist. She arrived at the house the next day to meet Davis. As soon as she got out of her car, she looked up at the house and the grounds and her expression changed to one of trepidation. *Something is definitely going on here,* she whispered to herself as she walked towards the door.

"Hi, nice to meet you- it's so good of you to come here so soon!" he said eagerly shaking her hand.

"Thank you, nice to meet you as well," she said as she entered the house and gazed from side to side. "Give me a moment to look around this house and we will chat some more," she said, smiling. She walked around looking very carefully at everything; her face was a mixture of solemnness and concentration. Davis followed just behind her. When they got down to the basement, Sandy suddenly looked very disturbed and quickly exited the room.

"I can't stay in there for long. There is too much of a disturbance of energy there. That is the place where the young girl died!" she said, gravely.

"I know, I was about to see it happen in my dream before I woke up," Davis revealed. Then he told her about the other dream and waking up in the other rooms. He also showed her the paintings.

"I think I see what is happening here," she finally said after a few minutes of silent contemplation. "This girl is attached to you for some reason. She sees something in you that she trusts. You are the only person that can help her," Sandy said as she shuffled her feet.

"Me? But why? How do you help someone who has already been murdered?" he asked, feeling quite puzzled.

"I don't know why she attached herself to you, but she needs help just like any disturbed spirit or energy. She cannot rid herself of what has happened to her in this life in order to transition to the next. She is destined to play out the horrors of her life over and over again until she can be freed of them. Let me attempt to communicate with her. Is there anything in the house that belonged to the girl?" she asked.

Davis went to get the wheelchair from the basement and brought it up to the living room. Sandy put her hands on it, closed her eyes and began to speak.

"Restless energy- whoever you are. Please speak to us. Share with us why you are still here and what we can do for you," Sandy said looking up towards the ceiling. A second later, the window nearest them flew open and then the girl's voice could be heard above them. It sounded like it was echoing in a dark cavern.

"NO! I will only share that with Davis!" she yelled and then suddenly the window shut. Sandy fell backwards and Davis rushed to catch her. The girl said nothing more.

"I'm afraid she doesn't trust me," Sandy said. "However, I think I know what you must do."

"What?" Davis said, "I'll do anything to help her and to get on with my work."

"Careful. Make sure that you free your mind of selfish motives- she can pick up on that. What you must do is engage in an intervention."

"Intervention? But how?" Davis said, obviously confused.

"The dreams you are having are no dreams. You are entering the portal to a dimension that exists on a different plane when you see these scenes that you call dreams. The girl's spirit has attached itself to you allowing you to see what she experiences in this plane. You are actually the 'essence' of yourself when you enter that plane. It is like your spirit self, instead of your usual self, in this plane," she explained.

"What the?" he said.

"I know it sounds strange, but what you must do the next time she brings you through the portal is intervene and try to help her. You can make contact with these figures you see when you enter that plane. Only you can do it because the girl has contacted you and allowed you to see what she experiences."

"Oh," Davis said, trying to make sense of it all.

"When you have helped her, contact me again and we will see what will need to be done next, if anything," she said, walking towards the door.

"Ok, thanks again," he replied, thinking to himself how apprehensive he was about having a violent struggle with an apparition.

"No need to thank me be careful and watch out for the other harmful energies that are present," she said as she exited.

Davis didn't have to wait long. That afternoon he took a brief nap on the couch hoping the girl would contact him. It took him quite a long time to get to sleep because of his growing apprehension at the thought of making contact with spiritual entities, but he finally drifted off. Just as before, he felt like had awaken from his nap; however, this time he realized what was happening. He knew it was no dream. Just as before he passed through the silvery curtain into the other dimension, he felt a tingling sensation all over his body. There again was the girl on the bed with the same forlorn expression, backing up against the wall as much as she could. He smiled at her and gave her a few words of reassurance.

"Don't worry; I'm going to put a stop to this. He will no longer be able to do this to you after tonight," he whispered reassuringly to her. "By the way, what is your name if you don't mind my asking?"

She smiled at him and said "Virginia," in a quiet, whispery voice. "Davis?" she asked.

"Yes?" he answered.

"Thank you," she said as a tear ran down her cheek.

"No need. I just want you to be free from all of this. No one should have to suffer through what you've suffered during your life; certainly no one should have to suffer through the same torment for eternity," Davis' voice grew louder as his anger grew at what she'd endured.

A second later, the man was entering the room again, giving off his distinctive smell of stale liquor and cigarettes. Davis slipped behind the dresser, waiting for the right moment. The man grinned evilly and approached the bed. Virginia crouched into a tight ball, trying to manipulate her useless legs with her arms. Suddenly, Davis emerged from behind the dresser and charged into the man. The old man was taken by surprise and fell backwards into a table. Unfortunately, this old man had some vim and vinegar left in him. He charged up to Davis and dealt him a blow across the chin. Davis moved backwards, but kept his footing. His face was now red with anger. He dealt the old man blow after blow across the face until he hit the floor, smashing his head against it. The old man fell out of consciousness, but Davis wasn't sure if he was dead. He couldn't tell if the old man was breathing. Davis turned for a second to check on Virginia

"Are you alright?" he asked as he smiled down at her.

"I'm fine," she said, "But you need to turn around NOW!"

Davis whirled around to face the old man; but he had already grabbed Davis' leg. Davis fell into some glass shelves, breaking them. Luckily he didn't have but a couple of minor cuts on him. He grabbed one of the wooden planks from the shelf and dealt the old man a serious and fatal blow to the head. Blood shot out from the side of the old man's mouth. He fell to the ground and did not move again. He turned and smiled at Virginia and she smiled back. Just then, he slipped out of the trance and exited the plane. He lifted his head.

That night, he slipped into a deep sleep like he hadn't experienced in several days. Davis thought that he had ended all of Virginia's torment that day, but it wasn't over yet. Again, he slipped into the dream-like state. This time he was quite puzzled as to why he was still entering the spiritual plane. Just as he had done during his second trip through the portal, he found himself in the basement and was watching the same scene play out again. There was Virginia in her wheel chair, again; he frantically began to speak to her.

"I don't understand Virginia," he said to her. "I thought I freed you from all of this when I killed that old man."

"Yes you did. I will never be violated by my uncle Frank again, but you have not freed me from my killer," she said. Then she screamed as she saw the shadowy figure approaching, just as it had over and over again each night. Davis turned and swung his fists at the figure, but his hands passed right through it. As he got closer to the figure, he realized that it was still a moving shadow with no form or expression that he could make out. It seemed unaware or unconcerned about him and it passed right through him on its way to attack Virginia. She screamed again and this brought Davis out of the portal. He sat on the basement stair, bewildered.

He contacted Sandy the next day and filled her in on everything that took place the night before. She thought long and hard after he told her about the shadowy figure in the basement.

"Well let's go over what we know," she said, "We know that the killer wasn't the uncle. We know that you can't make contact with the killer on the spiritual plane…" she went on.

"What if her killer is still alive somewhere?" he suggested.

"I think that is the case!" she said. "But who?"

"I wish I knew," Davis said. "Please give me a call if you get any ideas about how I should proceed with this," he said, ready to get off the phone.

"Well, we need to know who also lived in the house with Virginia and who else she might have had contact with," she suggested.

"Well Mary Walton lived here. Perhaps she is the aunt," Davis suggested.

"Could be. You need to find out what you can from her without being too suspicious," Sandy said. "Meanwhile, let me see what I can dig up through some research. Goodbye and good luck Davis!" He called Mary Walton that afternoon and asked if she could bring some more linen because he was having a relative come visit. She agreed to come by the next day.

"Thank you. Goodbye," he said as he hung up the phone.

He tried that night to get to sleep; but could not. Finally as the first light of day appeared he yelled up at the ceiling,

"TELL ME VIRGINIA! WHO IS IT? HELP ME SO I CAN HELP YOU!"

"Here! Bring a shovel!" he heard a voice coming from outside the house. He got dressed, grabbed a large shovel from the tool shed and went out to the back garden.

"This way!" he heard Virginia's voice again coming from the woods beyond the garden. He went down a narrow pathway through the woods as the light of day grew by the second. Again he heard her voice coming from beyond the bend in the creek. He crossed it and heard her voice again, still further into the woods. Finally he reached a rocky outcrop. Just beyond that he heard Virginia again saying,

"Right here beyond the rock pile. Dig!"

He did as she asked and about twenty minutes later, he came across a bag that was tied at the top. He took it out and untied it. He reached in the bag and pulled out a leg bone. Quickly, he dropped it back in the bag and tied it.

"That's what's left of me," Virginia said, "but there's more. Keep digging, just to the right of where you found my body."

After a couple of minutes he had found a small box. Inside the box was an old Remington with the initials F W engraved on it.

"Frank Walton," he said out loud.

"That's right," Virginia answered, "but it wasn't Uncle Frank that pulled the trigger!"

"I know that much. Who was it?" Davis asked, becoming impatient as he put the Remington in his back pocket.

At that moment, Mary Walton drove up. Virginia went silent. Davis heard the car coming, grabbed the shovel and ran out of the woods towards the house. He was walking up to the driveway when Mary got out of her car.

"What are you doing off in the woods?" she asked as he walked up. Just as she asked this, the Remington fell out of Davis' back pocket onto the ground behind him. When Mary saw this, her eyes took on a totally different expression. Her forehead wrinkled up as she gave off a hostile glare. That's when it dawned on Davis that Mary Walton was the killer; only he didn't know why she had killed the girl.

Mary tried to play it off like she didn't know why he had the gun and the shovel.

"What are doing with that gun and that shovel Mr. Davis?" she asked, reaching slowly into her purse.

"I think you know!" he answered. She suddenly pulled her hand out of her purse revealing a can of mace. She sprayed Davis right in the face. He yelled and fell backward, rubbing his eyes as he writhed about on the ground. Mary grabbed the pistol and stood over him.

"You need to mind your own business, Mr. Davis," She said.

"Now you force me to do something I haven't done in a long time," she said as she reached in her purse and pulled out a small handgun.

"So let me guess," Davis said as he attempted to look at her through his watery eyes, "You killed her out of jealousy, pure and simple. Not only did you not have the guts to help your niece and stop here from being violated night after night, but you hated her because she was the object of your husband's lust and not you. "

"ENOUGH!" she shouted as she pointed the gun at him, preparing to fire.

He rolled over suddenly and grabbed the shovel. She misfired, giving him enough time to jump up and deal her a blow. Her second shot went up in the air as she fell backwards. Blood ran from the wound in her head.

About a half hour later the police arrived and David told them as much as he thought they would believe. He told them that he had found the gun and the body, and the part about Mary Walton driving up and attacking him. He gave no mention about the apparitions or the portals or the voices….. The sergeant decided there were too many unanswered questions and they took him to the police station for further questioning. After a long hard session, they finally let him go. His story seemed to match the evidence. Davis went back to the house to gather his things and see if he could say his final goodbyes to Virginia. There was still crime scene tape surrounding the spot in the garden where Mary Walton died.

David went in and looked around the house. It was as silent as it could be; it was as if the whole business really were some kind of a dream.

"Virginia?" he said as he sat down on the couch, "Can you hear me? I just wanted to say goodbye."

He did this for several minutes; but he got no answer from Virginia. Finally, he nodded off where he sat. Again, he entered a dream-like state and was drawn to the basement where he would enter through the silvery curtain that tickles all of your nerves. Again, he saw Virginia in the wheelchair and a figure approaching form the right. Only, this time he could see the face of a younger Mary Walton, half cast in shadow holding her gun in front of her. His work to free Virginia from her plight was not finished.......

Made in the USA
Middletown, DE
18 May 2016